Rent a Friend

Rent a Friend

FRIEDA HUGHES

Hodder Children's Books

a division of Hodder Headline Limited

Chapter One

Danny walked into the pet shop. The bell on the back of the door rang as he closed it behind him and a tall, thin, grey-haired old man peered at him from behind the counter.

"I'd like to look around, if it's all right," said Danny in a small voice.

The old man nodded and went back to scribbling in his notebook.

5

There were rows and rows of cages all stacked up on top of each other against the wall, full of rabbits and guinea-pigs, rats and mice, kittens and puppies, parakeets and budgies and even a pair of chinchillas.

Danny walked slowly from one cage of furry bodies to another.

"Looking for something in particular?" asked the old man suddenly. Danny noticed he had a squint in one eye.

"Um, well, er, I was thinking of a dog," he replied uncertainly.

"Any particular kind of dog? A short dog? A long dog? A fat dog? A skinny dog? One with spots, or stripes, or plain?"

"Just any dog, a dog that could keep me company. I wanted to ask how much the puppies cost."

"It depends," said the man, widening his squinty eye for a moment. "You see, all the dogs here cost two months' pocket money, whatever that might be."

"You mean, if I was given a lot of pocket money in two months a dog would cost a lot, and if I was given hardly anything, then that would be enough too?"

"Got it in one," the man replied. "If you want a dog that's all yours, you have to pay for it. Two months' pocket money means you are serious and you'll look after the animal properly."

Danny had to agree this sounded sensible, though it didn't help him much. His father didn't give him pocket money and even if he did, it would be two months before he could buy a dog. And he wanted something to keep him company *now*.

"But a dog's not really what you want, is it?" said the shopkeeper.

"What do you mean?"

"You want someone to go places with you, to do things with you; you want a friend."

Danny blushed. "It would be nice to have someone to talk to after school," he admitted, "instead of just my sister. She's older than me. Besides, she has her own friends and all they want to do is buy clothes and wear make-up. There are people I like at school, but I never know how to talk to them."

"I'll tell you what," said the shopkeeper, "I don't just sell pets, there's another service I provide too: I hire out people. I can rent you a friend. You tell me the kind of friend you'd like, and I'll go through my records to find the right one. If they don't prove satisfactory, just tell me and I'll send you a replacement."

Danny stood in astonished silence, staring up at the long face and the squinting eye for a minute before he could bring himself to say anything.

"How much does a friend cost then?"

"Whatever you have in your pocket will pay for a week."

Danny emptied his pockets on to the counter. There were a few coins, a stick of chewing gum, three marbles and a ball of fluff. The shopkeeper gave him back the fluff. "You can keep that," he said with a smile. Then he scooped the marbles and change into a drawer behind the counter, unwrapped the chewing gum and put it in his mouth.

"Now," he said, bending over so he could study Danny more closely, "what kind of friend would you like?"

"One I could talk to," Danny replied. "Who would talk to me too. Someone I could go round town with. Someone who would help me build a tree house in the back garden. I've always wanted one, but it's no fun if you can't share it. Someone friendly. Someone who's fun to be with."

"Okay, I'll send someone round to you in the next two days. Just leave me your address and the name of your school so he can find you. If you get on with him, you get to keep him for nothing."

"How do I know I can trust you?" Danny asked.

"You don't," replied the shopkeeper, tapping the side of his nose. "But I know you can. My name's Arthur, by the way." He stuck out a slightly grubby long-fingered hand and shook Danny's hand.

Chapter Two

Danny left the shop with a doubtful look on his face. Was it really possible to rent someone? All he could do was go home to wait for his friend to arrive.

Minutes passed slowly and hours were worse. Lunchtime arrived but Danny couldn't eat and he didn't feel much like talking.

He couldn't concentrate on anything; he tried reading a book, he tried playing with the computer he shared with Katie, he tried sketching the fruit in the fruit bowl, he even cut the newspaper into strings of little paper people, but he didn't dare leave the house in case he missed his visitor.

He wouldn't know if Arthur had been telling the truth for another day and a half and, worse than that, perhaps he should allow an extra day in case there was some kind of delay?

When it got to nine o'clock Danny knew there was no one coming. But there was still tomorrow.

Next day there was a ring at the doorbell. Danny was there before the last tone had died away. On the doorstep stood a boy about his own age, with a mop of curly hair, big brown eyes and wearing an old anorak.

"Did Arthur send you?" Danny asked. The boy looked puzzled.

"Who's Arthur? I'm just looking for my cousin. He used to live here. His name is Peter. I don't suppose you know any Peter, do you?" Danny had to admit he didn't.

He was about to shut the door when it occurred to him that the rented friend might not know that's what he was. After all, a friendship would be much more authentic if it happened naturally, once Arthur had decided who was most suitable.

Danny invited the stranger in, and found out his name was Paul. Paul had just moved into the area.

"Arthur is as good as his word," Danny thought to himself. Here was someone who knew no one else except him. Paul was even going to start at Danny's school the next day. It was all too much of a coincidence – Paul just *had* to be the one.

At school, Danny made sure Paul sat with him. He was reluctant to introduce Paul to anyone in case they stole him away, but at the same time, he wanted to show him off.

However, Paul introduced himself to everyone, and everyone liked him. He was invited to a skateboard competition because he said he wasn't too bad at it, to go fishing with the "big four" who considered themselves better than everyone else, to a dance by one of the bolder girls who giggled a lot, and to a birthday party that everyone except Danny appeared to be going to.

Danny felt horribly jealous. Each time Paul was invited somewhere, he asked if Danny could come along, and the answer was always "yes", but Danny didn't really feel invited at all.

In an effort to find something just he and Paul could do together, he suggested they start building the tree house.

Paul thought it was a great idea, but it never happened. Too many people wanted him to do other things.

Danny watched Paul win the skateboard competition. He watched Paul catch the biggest fish although he swore he'd never fished before. He watched Paul dance really well, without a trace of self-consciousness. He watched Paul talk at the party and make people laugh.

By the end of the week, Danny was fed up with watching Paul. He liked him very much, but so did everyone else, which meant they were always in a crowd.

Chapter Three

"It was no good," Danny told Arthur.

"Was he nice?"

"Yes."

"Was he good company?"

"Yes."

"Was he friendly?"

"Very."

"So what was wrong?" asked Arthur finally.

Danny told him. "I think I need a friend who isn't quite so popular," he explained. "Someone who is more likely to spend time with me."

"I'll see what can be done," smiled Arthur, who didn't seem the least disheartened. "Now turn out your pockets."

This time Danny had more change with him. He reckoned that Arthur had made a real effort and deserved it.

Danny went home to wait as before. Only this time he wasn't so agitated. Now, he was sure his friend would arrive.

On Monday morning Paul wasn't at school. It seemed his father had been offered a good job somewhere else, and Paul had been taken away quickly to give him time to settle into the new school before half-term.

But Kevin was there. He was made to stand up in front of the whole class and tell them about himself. He was pale, almost as white as paper, with huge blue eyes, pale hair and pale lips. Danny wondered if there was something wrong with him – he looked almost as though someone had tipped a bag of flour over his head.

"I'm just over here from the States," announced Kevin in a quiet drawl.

"No you're not," thought Danny with a smile. "You're from the pet shop down the road!"

"My Dad always takes me with him when he works abroad, he says it's good experience," continued Kevin mournfully.

"How long will you be here?" Danny asked him at break time.

"Don't know," answered Kevin. "It could be a week or a year. I just kinda follow Dad around the world. This is my fourteenth school so far."

"Does that mean you make friends easily?" asked Danny cautiously. Kevin told him it was quite the opposite, which made Danny smile and invite him home for supper.

But when Danny asked if Kevin would like to help him build a tree house in the back garden, Kevin said he didn't like getting splinters and couldn't stand heights.

By the end of the week even Danny's mother was going crazy. "Why doesn't he ever invite you round to *his* place?" she wailed. "Every time I look, there he is. At breakfast to walk to school with you, at tea time because he walked back with you, and every day because he likes you. Couldn't he like you a little less?"

"It's because his Dad is never home and he's lonely," explained Danny, wishing that Kevin would fall down a hole and vanish.

If Danny said he wanted to go home and quietly read a book, Kevin would follow him back and read a book too. If Danny wanted to go for a walk by the river then Kevin wanted to go too. If Danny wanted to go to the bathroom, Kevin suddenly needed to go too.

Not only that, Kevin really had nothing much to say for himself. He was boring. Worst of all, he lived next door.

It was back to the pet shop.

"No good, huh?" asked Arthur, crossing something out in his notebook. Danny shook his head and turned out his pockets again.

"This one was too clingy and hardly spoke at all," he sighed.

"I need someone who isn't as popular as Paul, but who isn't as dull as Kevin. Someone who will help me build the tree house and isn't afraid of getting splinters."

"You're exhausting my supply!" cried Arthur good-humouredly. "Most of the others are variations on the theme."

"There must be *someone*," pleaded Danny.

"Do you really need someone now?" asked Arthur slyly. "After all, you don't seem to have any trouble talking to people any more. From what I've heard, you could get on quite well by yourself."

Danny stopped and thought for a moment. It was true, he was getting on much better with the other kids at school.

Danny turned out his pockets on the counter. "I'll have one last try," he said decisively.

Chapter Four

He wasn't sorry when he got home, to find a "for sale" sign up next door.

The new family moved in the following day. Danny was amazed at how quickly Arthur got things arranged.

But his face fell when he saw their new neighbours. The family consisted of a mother and her two children, a boy and a girl. The boy was in a *wheelchair*.

Surely his new friend couldn't be the girl?

He decided to wait for something to happen. Perhaps these people weren't the right ones? Perhaps the new friend would find him at school as Kevin had done?

But it wasn't so. The two children next door were the only new kids in his class. They were twins, though they didn't look at all alike.

They sat together in the lunch break at a table on their own. Danny took his tray over.

"Mind if I join you?" he asked politely. The two newcomers looked up and smiled. Their names were Sarah and Stephen.

"Do you know anyone who owns a pet shop?" asked Danny. They shook their heads and looked blank. But then that didn't mean anything.

He felt hopelessly confused. A girl wouldn't want to do all the things he wanted to do, and a boy in a wheelchair couldn't.

Stephen wheeled himself away from the table with his tray on his lap. He propelled himself towards the cart where they stacked the empty trays and plates.

"I'll do that for you!" cried Danny, leaping to his feet.

"That's very kind of you," replied Stephen, "but I can manage."

"He's very independent," whispered Sarah.

"How can he be?" asked Danny, watching as Stephen clumsily stacked his tray on the cart.

"He can't rely on people all the time," said Sarah, "so he does what he can for himself."

Danny walked home with them. Stephen wheeled himself alongside his sister and only when they got to a steep hill did he ask for her help. Danny took hold of the handle bars.

"You know, if you tell me when you need a hand," he informed Stephen, "I'll be glad to help. It'll stop you getting mad at me for offering to help all the time when you don't need it."

Stephen laughed. "Thanks," he said. "It's nice if you can be frank about it. Most people drive me nuts. They usually only offer to help because they feel sorry for me, and they're terrified that if they mention my chair I'll be offended. If it wasn't for the chair I really would be stuck. I just have wheels instead of legs!"

Danny thought it was a great pity they couldn't play football together, and a tree house would be out of the question. Perhaps Sarah played football?

This time Arthur had got it wrong. Really wrong. Stephen might be nice but he was a dead loss at being an active friend.

Chapter Five

Danny didn't ask his mother if he could invite Stephen round for supper. But Katie asked Sarah so Stephen came anyway. Danny sighed. The evening was going to be spent with someone who just couldn't do ordinary things.

"Now you've eaten, why don't you take Stephen up to your room?" Danny's mother asked him before she could stop herself. She quickly put her hand over her mouth.

"I'm sorry, Stephen, I didn't think," she gasped.

"That's all right," he grinned. "It's nice to know you forgot about the wheelchair! Actually, I'd like to go and see Danny's room."

Reluctantly, Danny led Stephen to the foot of the stairs. "Shall I see if I can carry you?" he asked, not knowing what else to do.

"Just watch," said Stephen.

He put the brakes on his wheels by the
handrail, and hauled himself out of the chair,
pulling himself at the same time on to the second
step from the bottom so he was sitting. Then
step by step he hauled himself up as if he was
doing backward press-ups, dragging his legs
behind him.

"Your arms must be very, very strong,"
commented Danny in admiration.

"It's from wheeling that chair all the time,"
smiled Stephen. "I learned that if I just had
patience, I could get myself in and out of most
places."

Once in Danny's room, Stephen propped himself against the edge of the bed and mopped his brow.

"Trouble is," he told Danny, "once I've got myself upstairs, I need to go down again for a drink!" They both collapsed in laughter.

"I suppose a tree house is out of the question?" asked Danny. They burst into peals of laughter again.

Danny was sorry when Stephen had to go. He might not be able to walk and run, but he was very good company.

Stephen wheeled himself round after school next day.

"What's that you've got there?" Danny asked curiously.

On his lap, Stephen had a large, heavy metal disk with a hole in the middle and hanging over his shoulder were several loops of rope.

"Before Dad died he used to lift weights," explained Stephen. "This is one of them. They gave me an idea for your tree house. There is also a pulley wheel in the bag on the back of my chair. I found it in the garage, the last people must have left it behind."

"But I was joking," protested Danny.

"I'm not, though," grinned Stephen. "If you come and help me get the rest of the weights and show me where you want your tree house, I'll tell you about it."

Danny looked up into the branches of the big tree at the bottom of the garden.

"Can you climb it?" Stephen asked him. Danny said he could, so Stephen gave him the pulley wheel. It was simply a wheel with a big pin through the centre and a metal holder that attached the pin on either side. Around the edge of the wheel was a deep groove and tied to a loop at the top of the metal holder was a bit of rope.

"Tie the pulley tightly to a branch just above where you want the tree house to be," instructed Stephen. Danny did as he was told.

Then Stephen threw him one end of the long rope he was carrying, and told him to thread it over the top of the pulley wheel so it hung down on both sides.

"There!" said Stephen. "Now all we have to do is tie me to one end and equal weights to the other. That way I will be able to pull myself up and down whenever I want to. I could pull myself up the rope without the wheel, but this will make it a lot easier."

"How much do you weigh?" asked Danny, laughing, looking at the kilos marked on each weight.

It took them two afternoons, but eventually they worked it out so there was a sort of harness affair that Stephen could just hitch under his arms, then he would pull down on the weighted rope so he rose out of his chair and up into the branches of the tree.

He had to do the last bit all by himself because by the time the weights were on the ground, he wasn't quite high enough, but the pulley made it easier. Then Danny could pull him on to the two big branches that were to support the floor of the tree house, before climbing down to pass up bits of the wood they were going to use.

Even if Stephen fell, he was safe; the weights would stop him before he got anywhere near the ground. "Just don't tell my mother!" he warned Danny.

By Sunday afternoon the floor was in place but the tree house was nowhere near finished.

That was when Danny realised he had completely forgotten to let Arthur know that he wanted his new friend to stay.

Chapter Six

Danny scrambled down the tree and ran across the garden. He hoped the pet shop was open on Sundays.

"Where are you going?" shouted Stephen.

"I have to see someone," Danny called back. "I don't want you to have to leave, but I might be too late!"

He ran all the way to the pet shop. "Please be open, please be open," he gasped under his breath. He swung around the corner and came face to face with the pet shop door.

There was a CLOSED sign on the window. Desperately, Danny peered inside. What if Arthur thought he didn't like this friend and took him away? He couldn't see anything. Not because the windows were dirty, but because there was nothing inside. No cages, no animals, no bags of bird seed and no Arthur.

"No! No!" he cried.

There was a newsagents next door. He hurried in and asked the fat lady behind the counter if the shop had recently closed down.

"Oh, my dear," she said sympathetically, "you must be new around here. It's been closed for two years. Everyone goes to the posh pet shop in the shopping centre now."

Danny turned and headed for home. He had a terrible sinking feeling that Stephen would have vanished by the time he got back.

He ran as fast as his legs could carry him. "Thank goodness you're still here!" he cried up to Stephen.

"Well, I had thought of running away," laughed Stephen from the branches of the tree, looking down at his wheelchair.

"No, no, I thought you might be moving away or something. After all, you're only renting the house next door until it's sold, aren't you?"

"That's what I've been meaning to tell you," Stephen grinned. "This morning Mum said we are going to buy the place ourselves!"

"But I heard her saying she couldn't afford it!" Danny pointed out.

"My uncle is going to help us. In fact, he's moving in," replied Stephen.

"You'll like him, he's fun. He looks a bit strange, but it's only because he's got a squint in one eye so you can never tell if he's looking at you properly. He's called Arthur. Now get up here and help me nail this wall together!"

HODDER

*These colour story books are short, accessible
novels for newly confident readers*

JOAN AIKEN
Winner of the Guardian Fiction Award
The
SHOEMAKER'S
BOY
Illustrated by ALAN MARKS

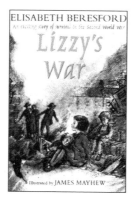

ELISABETH BERESFORD
An exciting story of survival in the Second World War
Lizzy's
War
Illustrated by JAMES MAYHEW

ELISABETH BERESFORD
the exciting sequel to Lizzy's War
Lizzy
Fights On
Illustrated by JAMES MAYHEW

LEON GARFIELD
Winner of the Whitbread Children's Book Award
Fair's
Fair
Illustrated by BRIAN HOSKIN

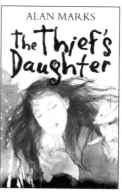

ALAN MARKS
The Thief's
Daughter

MICHAEL MORPURGO
Winner of the Smarties Prize
THE KING IN
THE FOREST
Illustrated by TONY KERINS

JILL PATON WALSH
By the Smarties prize-winning author of Thomas and the Tinners
Birdy and the
Ghosties
Illustrated by ALAN MARKS

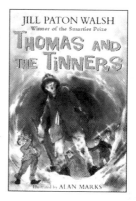

JILL PATON WALSH
Winner of the Smarties Prize
THOMAS AND
THE TINNERS
Illustrated by ALAN MARKS